MY
DEAR
LITTLE
ROOM
내 작은 방

박
노
해
사
진
에
세
이

04

MY
DEAR
LITTLE
ROOM
내 작은 방

PARK NOHAE PHOTO ESSAY 04

느린걸음

내 작은 방은 내가 창조하는 하나의 세계다
여기가 나의 시작, 나의 출발이다

My little room is a world that I create
This is my beginning, my starting point

CONTENTS

내 작은 방

우주宇宙는 집우宇, 집주宙. 나의 집은 우주다.
이 가이 없는 우주 가운데 지구 위에서
나 하나, 인간이란 존재는 얼마나 작은가.
단 한번, 인생이란 시간은 얼마나 짧은가.

우리 모두는 어머니 자궁의 방, 세상에서 가장 작지만 가장 위대한 방에서 태어났다. 그리하여 기쁨과 슬픔으로, 사랑하고 이별하고, 성취하고 저물어가면서 마침내 우리는 대지의 어머니, 땅속 한 평의 방으로 돌아간다.

살아있는 동안 한 인간인 나를 감싸주는 것은 내 작은 방이다. 지친 나를 쉬게 하고 치유하고 성찰하고 사유하면서 하루하루 나를 생성하고 빚어내는 내 작은 방. 우리는 내 작은 방에서 하루의 생을 시작해 내 작은 방으로 돌아와 하루를 정리하고 앞을 내다본다. 그곳에서 나는 끊임없이 새롭게 재구성되고 있다.

광대한 우주의 별들 사이를 전속력으로 돌아나가는 지구의 한 모퉁이에서, 이 격변하는 세계의 숨 가쁨 속에서 깊은 숨을 쉴 나만의 안식처인 내 작은 방. 여기가 나의 시작, 나의 출발이다.

국경의 밤이 걸어오고 여명의 길이 밝아올 때, 나는 세계의 토박이 마을과 그 작은 방들을 순례해왔다. 흙과 돌과 나무로 지은 전기도 없는 어둑한 방이지만 자기만의 터무늬와 기억의 흔적과 삶의 이야기가 흐르는 방, 가족과 친구와 차를 마시고 빵을 나누며 탁 트인 삶의 생기로 가득한 방들이었다.

아이들은 집안에 아로새겨진 가풍家風과 미풍美風, 그 기운, 그 성정, 그 정령, 그 마음의 파동에 감싸여 자라고 그것은 고유한 내면의 느낌과 태도로 스며든다. 그리고 야생의 대지에서 뛰놀고 일하고 모험하고 꿈꾸고, 여러 세대 가운데서 배우고 야단맞고 격려받고 어우러지며 함께 사는 세상에 대한 공동의 감각과 인간의 도리를 키워간다.

오랜 인류 역사에서 세계의 민초들은 작은 방에서 거처해왔으나 선조로부터 물려받은 공용의 공간과 대자연을 삶의 무대로, 더 큰 초원과 산맥과 고원을 누비며 살아왔다.

돌아보면 내 방이 커질수록 우리 삶의 영토는 점점 축소되고 있지 않은가. 세상에 좋고 비싼 모든 것을 내 집, 내 방 안으로 끌어모으고 있지 않은가. 카페와 바, 레스토랑, 영화관, 체육관, 스파, 전시장, 사무실까지 다 갖춘 나만의 작은 성에서 영주로 살고 싶은 꿈들이 각축하고 있지 않은가.

그럴수록 강인한 야생의 감성과 다양한 인간의 감각이 퇴화되어 편리한 만큼 무기력하고 세련된 만큼 차가워지고 진보한 만큼 획일화되고 접속된 만큼 고립돼가는 우리 시대의 날카로움과 위태로움을 강하게 느끼곤 한다.

더 슬픈 현실은 도심의 방세가 너무 너무 비싼 것이다. 그런데도 햇살도 들지 않고 테라스도 마당도 없고 나무 한 그루 꽃과 채소 한 포기 기를 수 없고, 그래도 좁고 불편한 방에 적응하고 정들 만하면 오르고 또 오르는 방세에 밀려 또 이삿짐을 꾸려야 하는 날들.

이제까지 내가 살아온 작은 방들은 내 조국의 식민지와 전쟁과 압축 성장과 급속한 민주 진보와 세계화와 정보화를 단숨에 질주한 이 땅의 역사와 모순이 응축된 방이고, 우리 시대의 저속한 안목과 삶의 가치관이 집약된 방이었다.

인간은 몸으로 사는 존재이자 욕망의 관계로 사는 사회적 존재이며 동시에 인간은 영혼을 가진 존재이다. 갈수록 소란하고 위험하고 급진하는 세계 속에서 나는 나 자신을 지켜낼 독립된 장소가 필요하다. 그러니까 진정한 나를 마주하는 내면의 장소, 내 영혼이 깊은 숨을 쉬는 오롯한 성소가 필요하다.

내 작은 방은 하나의 은신처이자 전망대이다. 이 은신처에서 나는 영혼의 파수꾼이 되고 상처 난 인간의 위엄을 가다듬어 세우고, 그 순간 이 은신처는 희망의 전망대로 전화轉化한다.

그러나 지금 시대는 내 고유성과 존엄성을 보존하기 위한 성소와 성역으로서의 방이 사라져가고 있다. 내밀한 은신처인 방은 투명한 유리창으로 변해버렸고 스마트한 기계들이, 온 세계의 유행들이, 쉼 없는 접속과 자극들이, 대중의 시선들이, 끝없는 비교와 우울이, 과시와 질시가 나의 내면까지를 관통하고 있다. 혼자 있어도 혼자 있지 않은 방. 내 영혼이 안식하지 못하는 방. 마지막 보루로서의 은신처가 사라지면 내 희망의 전망대도 사라진다.

내가 감옥 독방에서 무기징역을 살아갈 때, 연이은 실패와 좌절 속에 몸부림칠 때, 지구의 끝 절벽에 홀로 선 심정일 때, 그럴 때, 내 작은 방에서 되뇌어온 말이 있다. "세계 속에서 곤경의 시운時運에 처할 때는, 스스로 깊숙이 뿌리를 내리고 지극한 경지에 머물러 때를 기다리며 오롯이 내 몸을 보존하라."(장자莊子)

인간은 세계가 다 점령되고 타락해도, 최후의 영토인 내 심신을 지키고, 있는 그대로의 진실한 나를 마주하는 자기만의 방을 지킬 수 있다면, 우리는 다시 소생하고 세상을 새롭게 만들어 갈 수 있다.

하루 일을 마치고 나는 방으로 곧장 들어가지 않는다. 천천히 주위를 거닐며 오늘 내가 한 일과 내가 만난 사람과 내 감정과 태도를 되돌아 본다. 멀리 검푸른 산들과 청아한 향기를 내주는 꽃들에 부끄럽고 슬프기도 하여 밤하늘을 바라보며 눈물을 흘리기도 한다.

그리하여 나는 방문을 나설 때면 마치 고귀한 이를 만날 듯이 하고, 아무도 없는 방으로 돌아올 때는 마치 그가 계신 듯이 한다. 비록 작은 방이지만 지켜보는 이가 없다고 함부로 할 수 없다. 신독愼獨, 홀로 있어도 삼가함. 신독은 정말로 중요하다. 홀로 있을 때의 모습이 진짜 자신의 모습이기에.

나는 방에 들어가면 몸을 씻고 편안하고 품위 있는 옷으로 갈아 입은 다음 책상에 앉는다. 이 작은 방 안에 누군가 나를 만나기 위해 기다리고 있음을 느낀다. 그는 내가 거듭 보고 읽는 책상에 놓인 몇 권의 책들과 오래된 물건들과 유품들과 내 몸의 상처들 속에서 걸어 나온다. 가만히 숨을 고르면 그분들이 내 사유와 묵상과 기

억과 영감 속으로 걸어와 심야의 정담을 시작한다.

앞서간 그이들이 수천 년 전 내게 써 보낸 두꺼운 편지인 그 책을 펼치면, 고요하고 치열한 '불꽃의 만남'이 시작된다. 어떤 밤은 수백 년을 걸어서 내게 온 작고 단아한 물건들이, 그림과 음악들이, 도구들이 한켠에 앉아 묵연히 나를 바라본다. '잘 받아 보았는가, 거기 담긴 세월을. 공들인 그 마음을. 알아보고 귀히 쓰니 고맙네. 더 좋고 아름다운 걸 낳아주게.' 어둡고 힘든 시대를 불꽃처럼 살다간 거룩한 현자와 성인들과 민초들과 시인과 창조자와 혁명가들이, 내 작은 책상 위의 촛불로 일렁이고, 내 안에서 무언가 미래의 기척이 들린다.

나에게 기습하듯 불운의 날들이 오고 막막한 시간이 다가오면, 내가 제일 먼저 하는 일은 내 작은 방의 불필요한 모든 것을 비워내는 것이다. 청소를 마치고 몸가짐을 단정히 하고 지금 나에게 벌어진 일들을 정리하고 성찰하며, 단호히 단념할 것들과 결연히 밀어갈 것들을 다짐한다. 나의 결단은 내 작은 방에서부터였다.

내 작은 방엔 없는 것이 많다. 텔레비전도 컴퓨터도 스마트한 것들도 없고 그림 같은 인테리어나 이렇다 할 가구도 없다. 내 방에 가득한 건 고요와 여백이다. 하지만 나만의 삶에 꼭 필요한 그 하나는 최선의 것을 택해 닳고 낡아 나를 닮아가며 빛날 때까지, 다시 고쳐 입고 오래 쓴다. '적은 소유로 기품 있게'. 이렇게 나의 마음과 기운과 내면의 느낌이 생동하는 이 방은 내가 창조하는 하나의 세계가 된다.

세상에서 벌어지는 모든 일들은 내 작은 방에서 비롯되는 것이니. 자기만의 방에서 일어나는 생각과 행위와 마음이 다음날 세계의 사건으로 드러나는 것이니.

고백하거니와 내 청춘의 방은 반지하 자취방이었고 공장 기숙사와 군대 막사의 침상이었고, 내 인생에서 가장 오래 산 방은 감옥 독방이었다. 그 세월이 그렇게 했다. 그때도 지금도 나는 늘 작은 방을 전전해왔다. 처소를 지고 여행하는 달팽이처럼, 별들 사이를 떠다니는 우주의 미아처럼.

정처 없는 유랑자로 국경 너머에 내가 기거했던 처소는 별 세 개도 다섯 개도 아닌 수억 개의 별이 쏟아지는 광야나 초원이었고, 그곳 토박이들이 내어준 부엌 한켠의 어둑한 방이었고, 폭음이 울리는 전쟁터의 전기도 수도도 끊긴 객실이었고, 소녀 게릴라들의 초소였고, 국경의 온기 없는 여인숙이었고, 만년설산 고원의 작은 돌집과 사막의 동굴집과 봉쇄수도원의 방이었다.

어쩌면 내 작은 방이 나를 큰 세상으로 이끌어낸 것만 같다. '작은 방에 안주하지 마라. 큰 집에 집착하지 마라. 걸어서 나아가라. 세상의 모든 길과 온 대지를 누비고 계절의 향기와 고귀한 것들을 누려라.' 그렇게 나는 다양한 문명과 생생한 삶들과 숨은 빛의 사람들을 만날 수 있었다. 그리하여 우리 사는 세상의 큰 고뇌와 큰 울음을 품고 거대한 적에 맞서 투쟁하고 노동하고 사랑하며 살 수 있었다.

오늘도 내 작은 방은 이렇게 말하는 듯하다. '잘 잤나요. 좋은 꿈 꾸었나요. 찌푸리지 마요. 지난 밤 추운 데서 떠는 사람들이 많았어요. 힘들어도 힘차게 일어나 씻고 밥 먹고 곱게 차려 입고 자, 세상으로 나가요 우리. 오늘도 좋은 배움이 있고 좋은 인연이 있을 거예요.'

아직까지 이 지상에 집 한 칸 없는 나는 '수처작주 입처개진隨處

作主 立處皆眞'으로 살기로 했다. 내가 어디에 처하든 그곳의 주인이 되어 살고, 내가 서 있는 자리에서 참사람의 숲을 이루리라.

'어찌할 수 없음' 투성이인 우리 인생에서 내가 '어찌할 수 있고' '어찌해야만 하는' 것은 내 마음 하나이다. 모든 것의 시작이자 목적지는 내 마음의 빛이고, 내 마음의 방으로부터다.

내가 살아온 그 좁고 어두운 방들 속에서도 푸른 하늘빛으로 나를 감싸주고, 어려움 속에서도 나를 생생히 살아있게 하고, 다시 일어나 걸어가게 한 내 마음의 방. 언제 어디서나 누구에게도 빼앗길 수 없고 좌우될 수 없는, 정돈되고 정숙하고 정연한 내 마음의 방. 결국 이 지구에서의 한 생은 신성으로 빛나는 내 마음 하나, 꺼지지 않는 사랑의 불로 타오르는 '내 마음의 방'을 위한 것이 아니었을까.

나에게 세상의 모든 것이 다 주어져도
내 방에 세상의 좋은 것이 다 채워져도
내 마음의 방에 빛이 없고
거기 진정한 내가 없다면
나는 무엇으로 너를 만나고
무슨 힘으로 나아가겠는가.
나의 시작 나의 귀결은 '내 마음의 방'이니.
이 밤, 사랑의 불로 내 마음의 방을 밝힌다.

2022년 1월
박노해

My Dear Little Room

宇宙 means the Cosmos. 宇 means house, 宙 means house.
My house is the Cosmos.
On Earth, in the midst of this boundless Cosmos,
I, one human being, am so very small.
So very brief, just once, the moment we call a human life.

We are each of us born out from the room that is our mother's womb, the smallest yet greatest room in the world. Thus, with joy and sorrow, love and parting, fulfillment, and demise, we finally return to Mother Earth, a tiny room in the ground.

It is my little room that envelops me as a human being as long as I live, my little room that generates and produces me day by day, giving me rest, healing me, contemplating me, and meditating on me. We begin each new day in my little room and return to my little room to wrap up the day and look ahead. There, I am constantly reconstituted anew.

My little room, my only refuge where I can take a deep breath in the breathlessness of this rapidly changing world, in one corner of the Earth that goes spinning at full speed among the stars of the vast universe. This is my beginning, my starting point.

As frontier nights fell and dawn roads grew bright, I make a pilgrimage to the world's native villages and their little rooms. It might only be a dimly lit room built of earth, stone, and wood, without electricity, but it was a room alive with traces of one person's own grounds, memories, and stories of life, rooms filled with the vitality of lives, drinking tea and sharing bread with family and friends.

Children grow up surrounded by family traditions and good habits, their energy, their nature, their spirit, and their heart's waves, which are inscribed in their homes, and those permeate them with unique inner feelings and attitudes. They play, work, have adventures, dream in the wild, and while they learn, are scolded, encouraged, and harmonized by various generations, they cultivate a common sense of the world in which they live together and of human morality.

In the long history of mankind, the grassroots of the world have lived in little rooms, but they have been living in a common space and nature inherited from their ancestors as the stage of their lives, traversing larger grasslands, mountains and plateaus as they lived.

Looking back, as the room has grown bigger, has not the territory of our lives been growing smaller and smaller? Surely I am gathering every kind of good and expensive thing in the world into my house, my room? Aren't our dreams competing, dreams of wanting to live as a feudal lord in our own little castle, equipped with cafes, bars, restaurants, cinemas, gyms, spas, exhibition halls, and offices?

The more the strong wild sensibility and the various human senses degenerate, making them as lethargic as is convenient, as cold as they are sophisticated, as uniformized as they are advanced, and as isolated as they are connected, the more I feel acutely the sharpness and precariousness of our time.

An even sadder reality is that rents in city centers are too expensive. Although we adjust to and grow fond of small, uncomfortable rooms where there is no sunlight, no terrace, no yard, no way of cultivating trees, flowers or vegetables, still there are days when we have to pack up and move due to ever-rising rents.

The little rooms I have lived in so far have been rooms where the history and contradictions of a land that has gone speeding without a break through my fatherland's colonization, war, compressed growth, rapid democratic progress, globalization and informatization were all condensed together, rooms where the vulgar perspectives and life values of our time were concentrated.

Humans are beings that exist with bodies, social beings that live with relationships of desire, and at the same time, humans are beings with souls. In an increasingly noisy, dangerous and radicalized world, I need an independent place where I can protect myself. So, I need an inner place where I can face my true self, a perfect sanctuary where my soul can breathe deeply.

My little room is a hideout and an observatory. In this hideout, I become a watchman of the soul, refining and establishing the dignity of a wounded human being, and in that moment, this hideout is transformed into an observatory of hope.

But in the present age my room is disappearing as a sanctuary and sacred space allowing me to preserve my individual personality and dignity. My room, that secret hideout, has changed into a transparent glass window, while smart machines, fashions from all over the world, endless connections and stimuli, the public eye, endless comparisons and gloom, ostentation and jealousy are penetrating deep into me. A room where I am not alone even when I am alone. A room where my soul cannot rest. When the hiding place as the last bastion disappears, the observatory of my hope also disappears.

When I lived in prison in solitary confinement under a life sentence, when I struggled through successive failures and frustrations, when I felt I was standing alone on the edge of the world, there was a saying I always repeating in my little room: "When you are faced with hardships in the world, take root deep within yourself, stay in the supreme state, wait for the right time, and simply preserve your body."(Zhuangzi)

Even if the world is occupied and corrupted, if humans can protect their mind and body, the final territory, and their own room facing their true self, we can revive and make the world anew.

After finishing the day's work, I don't go straight into my room. As I slowly walk around, I reflect on what I have done today, the people I have met, and my feelings and attitudes. I am ashamed and sad as I face the distant dark blue mountains and the flowers that give off a pure fragrance, and I cry while looking at the night sky.

So when I go out, I feel as if I am about to meet some noble person, and when I come back to my empty room, I act as if he is there. Although it is a little room, I cannot act thoughtlessly only because there is no one watching me. Integrity, self-restraint, even when alone. Self-restraint is really important. Because the way you look and act when you are alone is your true self.

When I enter my room, I wash, change into comfortable and dignified clothes, and sit down at my desk. I feel that someone in this little room is waiting to meet me. He emerges from the few books lying on my desk that I keep reading over and over, old objects and memorabilia, and the scars on my body. When I take a deep breath, he walks into my thoughts, meditations, memories, and inspirations, and start a late-night chat.

When I open a book, a thick letter that my predecessors wrote and sent me thousands of years ago, a quiet and fierce "meeting of flames" begins. Some nights, small, graceful objects, paintings, music, or tools that have walked for hundreds of years to reach me, sit on one side and silently look at me. 'Did you read it properly? The years contained there, the painstaking heart. Thank you for recognizing it and using it preciously. Now give birth to something better and more beautiful.' The holy sages, saints, simple folk, poets, creators, and revolutionaries who have lived like flames through dark and difficult times shimmer like candles on my little desk, and I hear something inside me like a sign of the future.

When unlucky days come and hard times approach suddenly, the first thing I do is empty out all the unnecessary things from my little room. After cleaning it, I correct my behavior, organize and reflect on the things that have recently happened to me, and make a resolution on what things to give up on and what things to resolutely push forward. My decisions arise from my little room.

There are many things that I don't have in my little room. There are no TVs, no computers, no smart things, no picturesque interior, no furniture. What fills my room is stillness and empty space. But the one thing that is essential for my own life is to choose the best thing and wear it out, wear it for a long time, wear it again and again until it shines like me. 'Gracefully with few possessions.' This room, in which my heart, energy, and inner feelings come alive, becomes a world that I create.

Everything that I do in the world comes from my little room. The thoughts, actions, and feelings that arise in one's own room are revealed as the next day's events in the world.

I confess that in my youth my room was a semi-basement rented room, a bed in a factory dormitory or a military barracks, while the room where I spent the longest time in my life was a prison cell. That's what those years did. Then and now, I've always been going back and forth between little rooms. Like a snail travelling around carrying its own house, like a cosmic lost child floating among the stars.

As an aimless wanderer, the places where I lived after crossing borders were a wilderness or a grassland where not three or five, but hundreds of millions of stars shone down, a dark room in a kitchen offered to me by the natives, a guest room on a battlefield echoing with explosions where electricity and water were cut off, a guard post manned by girl guerrillas, an inn without any of the warmth of a frontier, a small stone house on a snowy mountain plateau, a cave in a desert, or a room in a cloistered monastery.

Maybe my little room always seemed to lead me toward the wide world. 'Don't settle down in a little room. Don't be obsessed with a big house. Advance on foot. Travel along all the paths and through all the lands of the world and enjoy the scents of the seasons and precious things.' In that way, I was able to meet various civilizations, vivid lives, and people of hidden light. In that way, I was able to fight, work, love, and live, struggling against the great enemy with the great anguish and weeping of the world we live in.

Today, my dear little room seems to say something like this. 'Did you sleep well? Did you have a good dream? Don't frown. There were a lot of people shivering in the cold last night. Even if it's hard, get up strong, wash, eat, dress up nicely, come on, let's go out into the world. There will be good learning and good relationships today.'

I, who have never owned a single house on this earth so far, have decided to live as "master everywhere, truth everywhere." Wherever I am, I will become the master and live there, and I will form a forest of true people wherever I stand.

In our lives full of 'It can't be helped,' my heart knows nothing but 'I can do it,' 'It must be so.' The beginning and destination of everything is the light of my heart, emerging from the room of my heart.

Even in the dark, narrow rooms I have lived in, the room of my heart has ever been enveloping me like the blue sky, enabling me to live in the midst of difficulties, enabling me to stand up and walk again. The room of my heart that is neat, quiet, and orderly, which cannot be taken away or swayed by anyone, anywhere, at any time. After all, wasn't each life on this earth, each heart shining with holiness, made for the sake of the 'room of one's heart' that burns with the fire of unquenchable love?

Even if I was given everything in the world,
even if my room was filled with all the good things in the world,
if there's no light in the room of my heart,
if there's no true me there,
with what will I meet you,
with what power will I move forward?
My beginning, my end, is 'the room of my heart.'
Tonight, the room of my heart is bright with the fire of love.

January, 2022
Park Nohae

빛 의 통 로 를 따 라 서

에티오피아의 고대 문명을 이어받은 성채 도시 곤다르.
세월만큼이나 깊은 어둠은 빛을 더욱 선명하게 한다.
우리가 먼 곳으로, 더 먼 곳으로 떠나려 하는 것은
바로 자기 자신에게 더 가까이 다가가기 위함이다.
오늘 현란한 세계 속에서 길이 보이지 않을 때는
더 깊은 어둠 속으로 걸어 들어갈 일이다.
어둠 속에서 빛을 찾는 눈동자가 길이 되리니.
내가 삼켜낸 어둠이 빛의 통로를 열어 줄지니.

FOLLOWING PATHWAYS OF LIGHT

Gondar, a fortified city that has inherited the ancient civilization of Ethiopia.
Darkness as deep as time makes the light brighter. In order to come closer to
ourselves we set off for places farther and farther away. In today's flashy world,
when we lose sight of the way ahead, it's time to walk into deeper darkness.
The eye that seeks light in the dark will become the path. The darkness
I swallow will open a pathway of light.

Gondar, Ethiopia, 2008.

LITTLE HOUSES ON THE GROUND

Villages with modestly sit inside small stone houses at the foot of the tall, rugged,
snow-covered mountains of the Andes. The tenacious labor handed down from
generation to generation, struggling step by step in the thin air, shines bright.
On plateaus close to the sky, everything is small. The people are small, the houses
are small, and supplies are small. But embraced by the Earth, how great is the love
that has been passed down from generation to generation in such high places.

Ancasi, Cusco, Peru, 2010.

지상의 작은 집

높고 험준한 안데스의 만년설산 아래
겸손하게 작은 돌집을 들어앉힌 마을.
희박한 공기 속에 한 걸음 한 걸음 분투하며
대대로 이어온 끈질긴 노동이 빛난다.
하늘에 가까운 고원에선 모든 게 작다.
사람도 작고 집도 작고 물자도 작다.
하지만 이렇게 높은 곳에서 대지의 품에 안겨
대를 물려 이어가는 사랑은 또 얼마나 큰가.

안데스 가족의 삶터

안데스 산정의 집터는 삶터이자 일터이자 놀이터다.
살을 에는 추위의 긴 밤이 지나고 태양이 떠오르면
온 가족이 저마다의 일을 시작한다.
아빠는 집 앞 비탈밭에서 감자 씨알을 심고
오빠는 알파카를 몰고 새 풀을 찾아 나서고
엄마는 눈 녹은 물에 빨래를 하고 햇살에 말리고
막내는 촐랑촐랑 뛰어다니며 심부름을 도맡아 한다.

THE BASIS OF AN ANDEAN FAMILY

A house high in the Andes is a home, a workplace, and a playground.
After a long, bitterly cold night, when the sun rises, each member of the
family begins their own work. Father plants potato seeds in the sloping field
in front of the house, the older brother drives the alpaca to find new grass,
and the mother washes clothes in melted snow then dries them in the sun,
and the youngest merrily runs errands.

Huancarani, Cusco, Peru, 2010.

해 맑 은 아 침 미 소

깊은 산마을에 여명이 밝아오면
나뭇단과 샘물을 지고 오는 건 소녀의 일과다.
부엌에서 아침밥을 짓던 엄마는
우리 딸 장하다고 애썼다고 웃음으로 맞아준다.
미소 띤 대화 속에 생명의 바람이 이는
'담소풍생談笑風生'의 아침이다.
미소는 인간이 가진 가장 아름다운 힘이니
서로에게 다정한 눈빛 한번, 해맑은 미소 한번,
새롭게 시작하는 하루가 눈부시다.

A BRIGHT MORNING SMILE

When day breaks in a remote mountain village, the little girl's daily task
is to fetch firewood and spring water. The mother, who has been cooking
breakfast in the kitchen, greets her with a smile, saying that she's proud
of her daughter for working so hard. It's a morning for engaging in lively,
cheerful talk, where the wind of life comes blowing in smiling conversation.
A smile is the most beautiful power that human beings have, so with a
friendly look exchanged, a bright smile, the new day begins, dazzling.

Palaung village, Kalaw, Burma, 2011.

손수 지은 인디고 흙집

기품 어린 자태의 그녀의 방에 초대를 받았다.
인디고와 흰빛으로 단장한 흙집 문을 열고 들어서자
나무와 꽃밭이 있는 정갈한 마당과 아름한 방이 있다.
누군가의 방 안에 초대받는 건 위대한 허용이다.
누군가를 내 방에 초대하는 건 위대한 포용이다.
그의 방을 보면 그의 안이 비쳐 보이기에.

A HANDBUILT INDIGO EARTHEN HOUSE

I was invited into the room of a graceful woman. Upon entering through the
door of the house decorated in indigo and white, I saw a neat yard, with trees and
flowers, and a correspondingly graceful room. To be invited into someone's room
is a great favor. Inviting someone into my room is a great gesture of magnanimity.
When you look into someone's room, you can see deep inside them.

Samthar village, Uttar Pradesh, India, 2013.

꿈 이 자 라 는 방

인디아에서 바느질은 가난한 여성이 배울 수 있는
손쉬운 기술이자 중요한 생계 수단이다.
오래된 재봉틀 한 대로 옷과 식탁보, 이불, 깔개 등
생활용품까지 직접 디자인해 만드는 지니(23).
먼 마을 사람들까지 솜씨 좋은 그녀를 찾아온다.
"제가 만든 옷은 세상에서 하나뿐이잖아요.
좋아해주는 사람들을 보면 저도 행복해져요.
언젠가 제 인생 최고의 작품을 만들고 싶어요."

A ROOM WHERE DREAMS GROW

In India, sewing is an easy skill and an important means of livelihood for poor
women to learn. Jinny(23) designs and makes clothes, as well as household
items such as tablecloths, blankets, rugs, with one old sewing machine.
Even people from distant villages come to visit her with her great skill.
"The clothes I made are unique in the world. Seeing people who like them
makes me happy too. I hope to make the finest work of my life someday."

Patha Karka village, Uttar Pradesh, India, 2013.

망고를 깎아주는 아버지

결혼한 딸이 첫 아이를 안고 찾아왔다.
아내를 떠나보내고 홀로 딸을 키운 아버지는
어두운 안색의 딸에게 아무것도 묻지 않고
딸이 제일 좋아하는 망고를 따서 깎아준다.
긴 침묵 사이로 눈물과 애정과 격려가 흐른다.
아내 사진을 바라보며 담배연기를 날리던 아버지는
딸에게 힘을 줄 닭죽을 끓이기 시작한다.
집이란 언제든 말없이 나를 받아주는 이가 있는 곳.
다친 새처럼 상처받은 존재들이 그 품 안에서
치유하고 소생하고 다시 일어서 나아가는 곳이니.

FATHER PEELING MANGOS

A married daughter came home with her first child. The father, who had sent his wife away and raised his daughter alone, does not ask his gloomy-looking daughter anything, but picks and peels his daughter's favorite mango. Tears, affection and encouragement flow through a long silence. The father, after smoking a cigarette while looking at a picture of his wife, starts to cook chicken gruel to give his daughter strength. A home is a place where there is someone who accepts me without saying a word. It is a place where wounded beings, like wounded birds, find healing and recovery in loving arms, rise and set off again.

Sukamukti, West Java, Indonesia, 2013.

A HOUSE OF SUNSHINE AND WIND

Even in the heat of the burning desert, the inside of the earthen house is cool
and pleasant. After a sand storm, the piles of sand are swept and wiped away, and
the white plastered walls are repainted again by hand to maintain cleanliness.
They plant and tend for the large shade-giving trees and flowers in the yard.
A house where the sun and wind pass in and out and the trees grow as the years
go by. A small but well-organized house that feels roomy and comfortable.
A vibrant house where a person, not a building or object, is the master.

Old Dongola, Nubian, Sudan, 2008.

햇살과 바람의 집

불타는 사막의 더위에도 흙집 안은 시원하고 쾌적하다.
모래폭풍이 불고 나면 수북이 쌓인 모래를 쓸고 닦고
다시 손으로 흰 회벽을 칠하며 정결함을 유지한다.
마당엔 커다란 그늘나무와 꽃들을 심고 가꾼다.
햇살과 바람이 드나들고 세월만큼 나무가 커나가는 집.
작지만 구성이 잘되어 여백미와 편안함이 느껴지는 집.
건물과 물건이 아닌 사람이 주인으로 생동하는 집.

자수를 놓는 소녀

혹독한 환경의 아프가니스탄 국경 마을.
엄마가 죽고 일찍이 살림을 맡은 소녀가
저녁 빵을 구울 아궁이 불을 피우고
장에 내다 팔 커튼에 자수를 놓는다.
"엄마가 이렇게 빨리 가실 줄 몰랐는데….
자수를 놓을 때면 엄마 목소리가 들려와요.
젊고 건강할 때 많이 배우고 익히렴.
더 의미 있는 일을 하고 더 많이 도와주렴.
젊을 때 젊음을 아낌없이 써야만
사람도 꽃으로 피어난단다."

A GIRL EMBROIDERING

An Afghanistan border village in a harsh environment. After her mother's death, a girl left in charge of housekeeping at an early age lights a fire to bake the evening bread and embroiders curtains to sell at the market. "I didn't know Mom would leave us so soon…. When I am embroidering, I can hear my mother's voice. You learn a lot while you are young and healthy. Do more meaningful work and help more. It's only if you use your youth unsparingly when you are young, that any human can bloom like a flower."

Drosh, Khyber Pakhtunkhwa, Pakistan, 2011.

창가에 핀 꽃 한 송이

'시베리아의 진주' 바이칼호의 알혼섬.

소련이 몰락한 이후 젊은이들이

도시로 빠져나가며 마을은 황량해지고 말았다.

아픈 노모를 위해 귀향한 나탸샤(21).

그녀 방 창가의 작은 풍경 하나가

얼어붙은 시베리아를 환히 밝힌다.

"그래도 우린 다시 일어설 거예요.

시베리아는 선하고 강한 사람들의 땅이니까요."

차가운 세상에 피워낸 선한 희망 같은

저 작은 한 송이 꽃이 가슴 시리다.

A FLOWER BLOOMING IN A WINDOW

Olkhon Island on Lake Baikal, the 'Pearl of Siberia.' After the fall of the Soviet Union, the young people fled to the city, leaving the village deserted. Natasha(21) returns home to care for her sick old mother. The landscape glimpsed from the window of her room shines, frozen Siberia. "But we will rise again. Siberia is a land of good, strong people." That one little flower like good hope blooming in a cold world makes my heart ache.

Olkhon, Lake Baikal, Irkutsk, Russia, 2005.

내 영혼의 동굴

계엄령과 휴교령이 내려진 카슈미르의 아침.
어른들의 긴장 어린 두런거림에서 빠져나온 남매는
전기도 없는 어둑한 방으로 숨어 들어간다.
한 줄기 햇살이 비추는 창가에 걸터앉은 누나는
글자를 모르는 동생을 위해 책을 읽어준다.
한 번도 가보지 못한 바깥세상과 아득한 별나라와
고대 신화 속으로 멀고 먼 여행을 떠난다.
인간은 누구에게나 자신만의 작은 동굴이 필요하다.
지치고 상처 난 내 영혼이 깃들 수 있는 어둑한 방.
사나운 세계 속에 깊은 숨을 쉴 수 있는 고요한 방.

THE CAVE OF MY SOUL

Morning in Kashmir, where martial law and school closures were imposed.
The siblings escape from the nervous murmuring of adults and hide in a dimly
lit room without electricity. The older sister, who sits by the window where a
single ray of sunlight shines in, reads a book to her younger brother who doesn't
know how to read. She embarks on a long and distant journey into an outside
world she has never been to, to distant stars and ancient myths. Every human
being needs their own little cave. A dark room where my weary, wounded soul
can dwell. A quiet room where you can take a deep breath in a wild world.

Wagnat village, Jammu Kashmir, India, 2013.

등불을 밝히며

라자스탄 사막이 붉게 물드는 시간,
이라폰(72)은 선조들의 사진과 물품을 놓아둔
선반 위에 등불을 켜고 하루를 마무리한다.
"나에게는 낮의 시간만큼이나 중요한 것이
내 마음을 밝히는 밤의 시간이라오."
밤은 그 사람의 진실한 모습이 비쳐 나오는 시간.
어둠은 그 내면의 은미한 빛이 비쳐 나오는 시간.
자기만의 방에서 일어나는 생각과 행위와 마음이
다음날 세계의 사건으로 드러나는 것이니.

LIGHTING A LAMP

At the time when the Rajasthan Desert is dyed red, Irafn(72) ends the day by lighting a lamp on the shelf where the photos and items of his ancestors are placed. "For me, the hours of the night, which illuminate my mind, are as important as the hours of the day." Night is a time when a person's true form is visible. Darkness is the time when the secret inner light shines through. The thoughts, actions, and feelings that arise in one's own room are revealed as the events of the world the next day.

Bairawas village, Rajasthan, India, 2013.

마 당 에 모 여 앉 아

원시의 풍경이 끝없이 펼쳐지는 파키르 마을.
원로 어르신이 평상과 의자를 놓아둔 이곳은
카페이자 회관으로 마을의 중심 장소가 되었다.
햇살과 바람이 좋은 날은 낮잠도 자고
여인들이 모여 앉아 수공예 작업을 하고
빵을 굽고 차를 마시고 아이들이 뛰어논다.
방은 작아도 공용의 터가 있기에 삶은 힘차다.

SITTING TOGETHER IN THE YARD

Fakheer village, where a pristine landscape spreads endlessly. This place, where the elders have put benches and chairs, has become the center of the village, serving as a cafe and hall. On sunny and windy days, they take a nap, while the women sit doing handicrafts, baking bread, drinking tea, and the children go running around. Although the rooms are small, life is strong because there is a common space.

Dohak Baba Fakheer village, Punjab, Pakistan, 2011.

A SPACE FOR YOUNG TREES

Raising a palm tree in a dry desert is like raising a child, it takes tremendous effort. You have to enclose a space with mud to keep out the strong haboob dust storms, bring Nile River water and pour it out every day. However, once the palm tree takes root, it grows magnificently, providing cool shade and sweet dates. The space that protects the young tree as it advances green, span by span, seems to be the small space that was our childhood room, no matter how barren, the best place to grow steadfastly.

Old Dongola, Nubian, Sudan, 2008.

어 린 나 무 들 의 방

메마른 사막에서 종려나무 한 그루 키우기란
아이를 기르듯 엄청난 공력을 쏟아야 하는 일이다.
진흙을 빚어 거센 하늄을 막아줄 방을 만들고
매일같이 나일 강물을 길어와 부어줘야 한다.
그러나 종려나무는 한번 뿌리를 내리기만 하면
장대하게 자라 시원한 그늘과 달콤한 대추야자를 선물한다.
한 뼘 한 뼘 푸르게 전진하는 어린 나무를 지켜주는 방은
아무리 척박하다 해도 꿋꿋이 자라기에 최선의 장소였던
우리 어린 날의 작은 방인 것만 같다.

사막의 아름다운 동거

문명의 끝 지점이자 황야의 최전선에서
인류의 지경地境을 넓혀가는 사막의 유목민들.
이곳은 너무나 거칠고 위험에 찬 곳이어서
소년은 어린 양을 한방에서 재운다.
어서어서 자라나 저 넓은 사막으로 나가자고
등을 쓰다듬어주는 소년의 마음을 아는지
어린 양은 고개를 숙이며 기분 좋은 울음을 낸다.

BEAUTIFUL COHABITATION
IN THE DESERT

The nomads of the desert are expanding the boundaries of mankind at the
forefront of the wilderness and at the end of civilization. This place is so wild
and dangerous that the boy takes a lamb into his room to sleep. As if it knows
the boy's feelings as he strokes its back, hoping they will both quickly grow up
and go out into the vast desert, the lamb bows its head and bleats in pleasure.

Cholistan Desert, Pakistan, 2011.

유 랑 자 의 노 래

자유와 유랑이 핏속과 뼛속에 스며있는 집시.

별빛을 이불 삼고 바람을 자장가 삼아 자란

집시 아이들의 눈빛은 야생 늑대처럼 형형하다.

가는 곳마다 핍박을 받으며 살아왔지만

날 때부터 새겨진 유랑의 충동은 막을 수 없다.

인생에서 가장 확실한 것은 대지와 밤하늘의 별빛,

자신의 두 발과 뜨거운 심장, 그리고 아이들이라는

삶의 진실을 춤추며 노래하는 존재들.

'나에게는 집도 없네. 기댈 곳도 없네.

온 우주와 대지가 나의 집이라네.

두 발과 어깨 위에 인생을 짊어지고

작은 천막에 잠시 쉬었다 떠나가네.

그 무엇도 아닌 자유만을 열망하며

그 누구도 아닌 나 자신을 살아가며

오, 어디에도 머무르지 말고 스스로 길이 되어 가라 하네.'

A WANDERER'S SONG

Gypsies whose freedom and wanderlust permeate their blood and bones. The eyes of gypsy children who grew up with the starlight as a blanket and the wind as a lullaby are glaring like those of wild wolves. They experience persecution wherever they go, but they cannot stop the urge to wander, which has been engraved in them since birth. The most certain thing in life is the earth and the starlight of the night sky, their own feet and hot heart, and the beings called children who dance and sing the truth of life. 'I have no home. There's nowhere I can rely on. The whole universe and the earth are my home. Carrying my life on my feet and on my shoulders, I rest for a while in a small tent then leave. I long for nothing but freedom, and I live my life. Oh, don't remain anywhere, become your own path and follow it.'

Hunza, Northern Areas, Pakistan, 2011.

라 디 오 를 켜 는 시 간

버마에서 가장 큰 강인 이라와디 강가에는
일용직 노동자들이 움막을 짓고 모여 산다.
대나무를 엮어 바닥과 천장을 만든 후
천으로 덮은 한 평짜리 방에서 살아가는 가족.
점심을 먹고 엄마가 동생을 재우는 사이
소년은 치직거리는 낡은 라디오를 켠다.
"저는 이 시간에 라디오를 듣는 게 젤 좋아요.
잘 들리지 않아도 그냥 이 소리가 반가워요.
아무도 나를 먼저 찾아와주지 않는데,
라디오에서 들려오는 목소리랑 노랫소리가
내게도 말을 걸어주는 것만 같고
여기를 넘어 세상과 이어진 것 같거든요."

TIME TO TURN ON THE RADIO

Day laborers live in huts along the Irrawaddy River, the largest river in Burma.
A family lives in a tiny room they covered with a cloth after making the floor
and ceiling by weaving bamboo. After lunch, while his mother puts his brother
to sleep, the boy turns on the old, crackling radio. "I love listening to the radio
at this hour. Even if I can't hear it well, I'm just happy with this sound. No one
comes to visit me, but the voices and songs I hear on the radio speak to me as
well, and I feel as if I'm connected to the world beyond here."

Mandalay, Burma, 2011.

FOR BABY LAMBS

The Indian women take care of the livestock that give fresh milk, fuel and manure every day like children, saying they are a gift from God. Under the scorching sunlight of the Rajasthan Desert, the woman made a basket out of bamboo to shelter the young lambs in the shade and to protect them from ferocious beasts. When it is time for them to feed and the basket is opened, the baby lambs run towards their mother in a row.

Gorisar village, Rajasthan, India, 2013.

아 기 버 끄 리 를 위 해

날마다 신선한 젖과 연료와 거름을 주는
가축은 신께서 보내신 선물이라며
아이처럼 정성껏 돌보는 인디아의 여인들.
라자스탄 사막의 이글거리는 불볕 아래
새끼 버끄리들을 그늘에서 쉬게 하고
사나운 맹수로부터 보호하기 위해
여인은 대나무로 바구니 방을 만들었다.
젖 먹을 때가 되어 바구니를 열어주자
아기 버끄리들은 어미를 향해 줄지어 달려간다.

세 상 에 서 제 일 작 은 백 화 점

지상의 집 한 칸 갖지 못한 이들이
밀려나고 떠밀려온 달라Dala 마을.
여기 '세상에서 제일 작은 백화점'이 있다.
천장에 매달아 놓은 작은 비닐봉지에는
소금, 쌀, 설탕, 식용유, 양념 등을 소분해
가난한 살림에 일용할 만큼 사 가도록 했다.
마을 소식이 가장 빠르고 정확한 이곳은
서로 돌보고 나누는 '작지만 큰 사랑방'이다.

THE SMALLEST DEPARTMENT STORE
IN THE WORLD

The village of Dala is a place where people without any house on earth have
been pushed out and driven away to. Here is 'the world's smallest department
store'. In small plastic bags hanging from the ceiling, salt, rice, sugar, cooking
oil, and seasoning are divided into small quantities so that the poor can buy
just enough for daily living. The quickest and most accurate news of the
village is heard in this 'tiny but vast guest-room' where people care for each
other and share together.

Dala, Yangon, Burma, 2011.

숲 속 의 목 욕 터

흙먼지 이는 길을 걸어 장터에 다녀온 아가씨들이
집으로 들어가기 전에 들르는 숲속 목욕터.
전통 의상 렁지를 끌어올려 가슴을 감싼 여인들은
건강하고 부드러운 어깨를 빛내며
흐르는 강물에 몸을 담그고 땀을 씻어낸다.
오늘 하루 좋았던 일, 나빴던 일도 다 꺼내 놓으며
행여 얼룩진 마음 구석까지 깨끗이 정화한다.

A BATHING PLACE IN THE FOREST

A bathing place in the forest where young girls who have walked along dusty
roads to and from the market stop before entering their homes. Women in
traditional costumes, pulling up their longyis to wrap their chests, bathe
in the flowing river water to wash off their sweat, shining healthy, soft
shoulders. They take out all the good and bad things of the day and purify
even the maybe-soiled corners of their hearts.

In Dein, Nyang Shwe, Burma, 2011.

톤 레 삽 의 수 상 가 옥

아시아에서 가장 큰 바다 같은 호수 톤레삽.

지상에 집 한 칸 마련할 땅조차 없는 가난한 이들이

출렁이는 황톳빛 강물 위에 뗏목 집을 짓고 살아간다.

누군가는 이곳에 태어나지 않았음에 감사를 바치지만,

싱싱한 생선을 잡아 올리고 액젓을 담아 제공하는

이들이 없다면 이 나라 밥상은 메마르고 말리라.

"저도 흙을 밟고 나무를 심고 살고 싶죠.

그래도 사랑하는 사람과 함께 있고

가족이 모여 웃으며 살 수 있다면

그곳이 땅인들 물인들 어때요."

FLORATING HOUSE IN TONLÉ SAP

Tonlé Sap, the largest sea-like lake in Asia. Poor people who do not even have land to build a house on the ground live in raft houses over the churning, ochre-hued river. Some might gives thanks for not having been born here, but if it were not for these people catching fresh fish, making fish sauce and serving them, the meal tables in this country would be barren. "I also want to live on the dry ground and plant trees. Still, if you can be with your loved ones and live happily gathered as a family, it does not matter if here is land or water."

Lake Tonle Sap, Cambodia, 2006.

난민 가족의 단칸방

이스탄불 외곽의 쿠르드 난민 가족.

전기도 없는 차가운 단칸방에 아홉 식구가 살아간다.

1992년 터키군은 마르딘에 있던 고향 집을 불태웠다.

"아이들이 풀 죽어 있을 때면 늘 말해요.

우린 지금 단칸방에 살지만 우리 각자가 고향의 나무가 되자.

강물이 되고 새가 되고 별이 되고 쿠르드의 아침 태양이 되자.

딸아 아들아, 고개를 들어라. 어깨를 펴라. 용기를 내라."

전사처럼 살아온 어머니의 눈시울이 붉어진다.

A REFUGEE FAMILY'S SINGLE ROOM

A family of Kurdish refugees outside Istanbul. A family of nine lives in one cold room with no electricity. In 1992, Turkish forces burned down their home in Mardin. "I always tell the kids when they feel discouraged. We live in a single room now, but let's each become a hometown tree. Become the river, the birds, the stars, the Kurdish morning sun. Daughter, son, raise your heads, straighten your shoulders, be brave." The eyes of the mother, who has lived like a warrior, brim with tears.

Istanbul, Turkey, 2005.

환대의 식사

걸어도 걸어도 끝이 없는 알 자지라 평원에
첫 비가 내리고 햇살이 눈부신 아침이다.
쿠르드 마을의 움미(어머니)는 낯선 나그네의 손을 이끈다.
레몬즙을 짜 넣은 신선한 양젖 요구르트와
후추를 갈아 넣은 허브치즈, 고추피클과 자두절임,
야생꿀과 올리브기름과 갓 구운 빵을 내온다.
여기 이 작은 방은 우리를 감싸주고 있고
세상 어디서든 너를 반기는 벗은 있다고,
속 깊은 그 마음이 은은한 햇살로 빛난다.

A MEAL OF HOSPITALITY

It is the morning of the first rains and the sun is dazzling on the Al Jazeera
plain, where there is no end no matter how far you walk. Ummi from the
Kurdish village leads the stranger by the hand. Fresh sheep's milk yogurt with
squeezed lemon juice, herb cheese with ground pepper, pickled red pepper
and prunes, wild honey, olive oil and freshly baked bread are served. This
little room surrounds us, and that deep heart shines like soft sunlight, telling
us that there is a friend ready to welcome you gladly everywhere in the world.

Tell Beydar, Syria, 2008.

A SECRET PERFORMANCE
BY KURDISH YOUTH

The Kurds, the world's largest ethnic minority, have lost their country and
are wandering. During a late-night performance, held in secret to escape the
Syrian government's surveillance, they take out hidden traditional attire and
sing in their forbidden language. Now, this room is a space of liberation for
the Kurds and the site of the independence movement. Even today, around the
world, oppressed and exiled people are struggling, even in small rooms, crying
for freedom. To be alive is to resist; in any case youth is singing and dancing,
loving and resisting and finding a way.

Al Qamishli, Syria, 2005.

쿠르드 청년들의 비밀 공연

나라를 잃고 떠도는 세계 최대의 소수민족 쿠르드.
시리아 정부의 감시를 피해 모인 심야의 비밀 공연에서
감춰둔 전통복장을 꺼내 입고 금지된 모국어로 노래한다.
지금 이 방은 쿠르드인들의 해방공간이자 독립운동 현장.
오늘도 세계 곳곳에서는 억압받고 추방당한 자들이
작은 방 한 칸에서라도 몸부림치며 자유를 부르짖고 있다.
살아있다는 것은 저항한다는 것이니,
어떤 경우에도 젊음은 노래하고 춤추고
사랑하고 저항하며 길을 찾는 것이니.

운전기사의 '트럭 아트'

폭음이 울리는 아프가니스탄 국경 산악도로
'로와리 패스'를 긴장과 피로 속에 달려온 화물기사.
"집에서 잔 날보다 이 차에서 잔 밤들이 더 많았지요.
나의 방이고 일터이고 제일 오래된 친구랍니다."
자신의 몇 년 치 월급을 들여 태양과 별, 산과 호수,
꽃과 나무를 그려 넣고 성전처럼 정성스레 장식했다.
그는 따뜻한 짜이 한 잔으로 몸을 녹이더니
금세 흙먼지 낄 트럭을 언 손으로 닦아준다.
이 일이 비록 밥을 버는 일이지만
그 모든 시간이 내 소중한 인생이고
이 인생길의 주인은 나 자신이기에.

A DRIVER'S 'TRUCK ART'

A cargo driver who has driven at high speed, tense and weary, along the Afghanistan border mountain road called "Lowari Pass" where gunfire echoes. "I have slept more nights in this truck than I have slept at home. It's my room, my work, and my oldest friend." He spent several years' salary having it carefully decorated like a temple, with drawing of the sun and stars, mountains and lakes, flowers and trees. He warms himself up with a cup of hot Chai and wipes the truck which was quickly getting dirty with his frozen hands. Although he does this job to earn a living, all the time it takes is his precious life, and he is the master of his life's journey.

Lowari Pass, Pakistan, 2011.

고 비 사 막 의 게 르

끝없는 초원과 황무지가 펼쳐지는 고비 사막.
사막에는 길이 없다. 가는 곳이 곧 길이다.
초원에는 터가 없다. 천막 방이 그의 터다.
한곳에 오래 안주하면 사람이 나태해지고
귀한 초원도 황폐해져 사막이 되고 말기에,
간소한 살림살이만 단단하게 이고 지고
내일이면 다시 새 풀을 찾아 길을 떠난다.
가이 없는 우주 가운데 지구에서의 짧은 한 생.
아, 나는 이 땅에 잠시 천막을 친 자이니
내가 걸어온 등 뒤에는 푸르름만 남기를.

A GER IN THE GOBI DESERT

Endless grasslands and wastelands of the Gobi Desert. There are no roads in
the desert. Wherever you go is the road. There is no dwelling place in the
grasslands. The tent is his dwelling place. If they stay put in one place for a long
time, people become lazy, and the precious grasslands become desolate and turn
into desert, so firmly carrying only a few simple belongings, he stops then sets
off again tomorrow in search of new grass. A short life on Earth in the midst
of an endless universe. Ah, I too am someone who have pitched my tent on this
earth for a moment, so I hope that I will leave green behind me as I journey on.

Gobi Desert, Mongolia, 2005.

엄마의 등

안데스 만년설산 자락의 감자 수확 날.
엄마는 뉘어놨던 아이가 추위에 칭얼대자
전통 보자기 리클라로 등에 업고 자장가를 불러준다.
우리 모두의 첫 번째 방은 엄마의 등.
찬바람 치는 세계에서 가장 따뜻하고 믿음직한
그 사랑의 기운이 내 안에 서려 있어,
나는 용감하게 첫 걸음마를 떼고
마침내 스스로의 힘으로 선 청년이 되어
나만의 길을 찾아 걸어가고 있으니.
사랑, 그 사랑 하나로 충분한 엄마의 등은
가장 작지만 가장 위대한 탄생의 자리이니.

MOTHER'S BACK

Potato harvest day at the foot of the snow-covered Andes. As soon as her child lying there whimpers for cold the mother lays it on her back wrapped in a Lliclla and sings a lullaby. Our mother's back is everyone's first room. The warmest and most reliable energy of love in a world where cold winds blow lies within me, so I take my first steps bravely and finally became a young man standing on my own feet and walking in search of my own path. Love, that love alone is enough for a mother's back to be the smallest but the greatest birth place.

Patacancha, Cusco, Peru, 2010.

WE HAVE A PLACE
WE MUST GO BACK TO

Sudan's black tears, Darfur. The genocide that continued for more than a decade from 2003 killed 300,000 people and made 2.7 million refugees. When the eyes of children who seem to have seen all the sorrows and tragedies of the world are immersed in the red sunset, after her daily work in an unfamiliar land, their mother comes home, prepares dinner, and comforts her children. "Darfur is the 'Land of the Fur.' Now your house is on a cold street, but we have a place we must go back to. We should not put out the spark of hope."

Al Qadarif, Sudan, 2008.

돌아가야 할 곳이 있어

수단의 검은 눈물 다르푸르.
2003년부터 10년 넘게 계속된 학살로
30만 명이 죽고 270만 명이 난민이 되었다.
세상의 슬픔과 비극을 다 보아버린 듯한
아이들의 눈동자가 붉은 노을에 잠길 때
낯선 땅에서 일용직을 마치고 온 엄마가
저녁밥을 차려주며 아이들을 토닥인다.
"다르푸르는 '푸르족의 땅'이란다.
지금 너의 집은 차가운 길바닥이나
우린 꼭 돌아가야 할 곳이 있단다.
희망의 불씨만은 꺼뜨리지 말아라."

하늘을 보는 아이

길어진 그림자가 이 세계의 경계를 넘어
심연에 가닿는 듯한 석양의 시간이 오면,
하루 일을 정리하는 식구들 사이에서
아이는 홀로 지붕에 올라 하늘을 바라본다.
점점이 밝아오는 별빛이 눈동자에 반짝이고
작은 몸 안에 고요히 무언가가 스며든다.
아이들에겐 혼자만의 비밀스런 시간이 필요하다.
여기는 어디인지, 나는 누구인지, 무얼 꿈꾸는지,
자기 안에 살아있는 신성이 깨어나는 시간,
어둠 속 별의 지도를 읽어가는 시간이 필요하다.

CHILD LOOKING AT THE SKY

When sunset comes, when the elongated shadows seem to cross the borders of this world and touch the abyss, the child climbs onto the roof alone and looks up at the sky among the family members who are finishing the day's work. The bright stars twinkle in his eyes one by one and something quietly seeps into his small body. Children need their own private time, where I am now, who I am now, what I am dreaming of now, the time to awaken the living divinity within me, and time to read the map of the stars in the dark.

Jaipur, Rajasthan, India, 2013.

짜 이 한 잔 의 기 쁨

오늘은 흙을 다져 방 한 칸을 새로 짓는 날.
솜씨 좋은 목수와 마을 청년들이 일손을 보탠다.
이 집만의 고유한 짜이 맛을 내는 건 어머니의 몫,
차를 대접하는 건 자기만의 방이 생긴 딸의 몫이다.
청년들은 그녀에게 잘 보이려 눈을 빛내고,
그녀는 무심한 척 두 손에 그득한 찻잔을 나르고,
고소한 짜이 향기와 함께 기쁨이 번져간다.

THE JOY OF A CUP OF CHAI

Today is the day to compact the soil and build a new room. Skillful carpenters and village youths help out. It is the responsibility of the mother to create this house's unique chai flavor, and the responsibility of the daughter to serve the brimming chai, now that she has her own room. Young men are alert to look good, and she pretends to be indifferent as she carries cups of chai in her hands, and joy spreads with the fragrant chai scent.

Gafa village, Rajasthan, India, 2013.

인 디 아 가 정 의 성 소

집안의 벽과 기둥에도 신이 깃들어 있다고 믿는
인디아 여인들은 아침이면 흰 쌀가루를 개어
풍요를 바라는 그림으로 부엌 벽을 단장한다.
샘물을 길어 오는 길에 향기로운 꽃을 꺾어 바치고
가족의 평안을 기원한 후 아침식사를 준비한다.
식구들의 정성과 기도가 깃든 부엌은
하루하루 생의 모든 것이 시작되는 성소이다.

THE INDIAN FAMILY'S SANCTUARY

Indian women, who believe that the walls and pillars of the house are also
inhabited by gods, use white rice flour in the morning to decorate the
kitchen walls with paintings praying for abundance. On the way to fetch
spring water, they pick fragrant flowers to offer, pray for family peace, and
prepare breakfast. The kitchen, where the devotion and prayers of the family
members reside, is the sanctuary where everything in life begins.

Auli village, Orissa, India, 2013.

두 손을 녹이는 노부부

긴 세월 한 길을 걸으며 기쁨과 슬픔을 함께 해온
노부부가 일곱 아이를 낳아 출가시킨 흙집 방에서
불을 피워 언 몸을 녹이며 아침을 맞이한다.
카스트 계급의 최하층민으로 태어나
저 두 손으로 얼마나 많은 노동을 하고
밥을 짓고 쓸고 닦고 아이들을 씻기고 안아주었을까.
저 두 손으로 얼마나 많은 씨앗을 심고 꽃을 기르고
눈물을 닦아주고 사무치는 기도를 바쳤을까.
이제는 젊음이 다 흘러나간 빈손이지만
오늘도 또 하루를 함께할 수 있어 감사한 생이라고
사랑으로 닳아진 서로의 손을 위로한다.

AN OLD COUPLE WARMING THEIR HANDS

An elderly couple, who have shared joy and sorrow while walking along a single road for a long time, welcomes the morning and warm their frozen bodies with a fire in the earthen room where they gave birth to and married off seven children. Born as the lowest class of the caste class, how much labor have they had to perform with those two hands, cooking, sweeping and wiping the floor, washing and hugging the children? How many seeds had been planted, how many flowers had been raised, how many tears had been wiped away, and how many prayers had been offered with those two hands? Now they are empty-handed, their youth is gone, but they comfort each other's hands, worn out by love, saying that they are grateful to life to be able to spend another day together today.

Patha Karka village, Uttar Pradesh, India, 2013.

LANDSCAPE WITH TABLE

Placing a table in the middle is to change the landscape of the house at once. When your loved ones are sitting around on comfortable chairs and the flowers of the seasons and warm sunlight shine, this is a place where you are invited to fresh joy and abundance. A place where a new world is born on earth.

Turkey, 2005.

탁자가 놓인 풍경

집안의 풍경을 단번에 바꿔버리는 것은
공간의 중심에 탁자 하나를 놓는 것이다.
편안한 의자에 사랑하는 이들이 둘러앉고
계절의 꽃과 따뜻한 햇살이 비추이면,
여기는 신선한 기쁨과 풍요로 초대되는 자리.
지상에 하나의 새로운 세계가 탄생하는 자리.

'둘씨' 기도를 하는 여인

인디아 민초들의 흙마당은
맨발로 다닐 만큼 반질반질 정갈하다.
집집마다 마당 한가운데는
둘씨 나무를 심은 성소가 있다.
'비교할 수 없는 것'이라는 뜻을 가진
둘씨는 5천 년 넘게 약재로 쓰였으며,
인디아인들은 사람의 마음을 열어
자비의 미덕을 불러일으킨다고 믿는다.
"집안의 중심은 성소이지요.
성소가 없는 집은 집이 아니지요.
마음의 중심에 사랑과 자비가 없다면
심장이 없는 사람과 같지요."
하루의 시작과 끝. 고요한 둘씨의 시간.

A WOMAN WHO PRAYS TO THE 'TULSI'

The soil forming the Indian yard is so smooth and clean that you can walk
barefoot. In the middle of the yard in each house, there is a sanctuary planted
with a Tulsi tree. Tulsi, meaning "incomparable," has been used as a medicinal
herb for over 5,000 years, and Indians believe that it opens people's hearts
and evokes the virtue of mercy. "The center of the house is a sanctuary.
A house without a sanctuary is not a house. If you don't have love and mercy
in the center of your heart, you're like a person without a heart."
The beginning and end of the day. A quiet Tulsi time.

Orchha, Madhya Pradesh, India, 2013.

THE LAST ROOM ON EARTH

The tomb in the Himalayas of a young man who died fighting for Kashmir independence. Since it is not yet possible to erect a tombstone, people plant daffodils and light candles every day for the young man who sleeps in a small room below the ground. Ultimately, we are all walking towards death. Someday, when I stand before death, what will I have wanted to do before I die? At whose side will I have wanted to die? The place I want to die is the place where I really want to live, so am I living the life I want to live right now in the place where I want to die? The nameless daffodil flowered tomb asks.

Waterwani village, Jammu Kashmir, India, 2013.

지상에서의 마지막 방

히말라야 산속에서 카슈미르 독립을 위해
총을 들고 싸우다 죽은 청년의 무덤.
아직 묘비 하나 세워줄 수 없는 처지이기에
땅속 한 평의 방에 잠든 청년을 위해
사람들은 수선화를 심고 날마다 촛불을 밝힌다.
우리 모두는 결국 죽음을 향해 걷고 있다.
언젠가 어느 날인가 죽음 앞에 세워질 때,
나는 무얼 하다 죽고 싶었는가.
나는 누구 곁에 죽고 싶었는가.
내가 죽고 싶은 자리가 진정 살고 싶은 자리이니,
나 지금 죽고 싶은 그곳에서
살고 싶은 생을 살고 있는가.
이름 없는 수선화 꽃 무덤이 물어온다.

고원의 발걸음

한 걸음만 걸어도 숨이 차는 높고 깊은
안데스 고원길의 보따리장수 델 솔라르(63).
멀리 떨어진 마을과 집들을 오가는 그의 등짐에는
밤이면 방이 될 천막과 담요, 식량과 요리 도구,
자녀와 친구에게 전해달라고 부탁받은
생일 선물과 편지들까지 가득 담겨있다.
"나이가 드니 점점 발걸음이 느려지네요.
하지만 저를 기다리고 반겨주는 이들이 있어서,
30년 넘게 해온 일을 누가 대신할 수도 없어서,
내 다리가 허락하는 한 이렇게 걸어야지요. 하하."
이 지상에 나만이 해야 할 일이 있다는 그 무게가
오늘도 나를 걷게 하는 힘인 것을.

FOOTSTEPS IN THE HIGHLANDS

Del Solar(63), a peddler on the high and deep Andean highland road that takes
your breath away with just one step. On his back as he walks to and from
distant villages and houses, he has the tent and blankets that become his
room at night, food and cooking utensils, even birthday presents and letters
which he has been asked to deliver to children and friends. "The older I get,
the slower I walk. But there are people waiting and welcoming me, and no
one can take over the work I have been doing for over thirty years, so I have
to go on walking like this as long as my legs allow it. Ha ha." The weight of
the knowledge of my duty, that there is work I alone have to do on this earth,
is the power that makes me go on walking today.

On the way to Colca valley, Peru, 2010.

THE ROOM OF MY HEART

I don't own a house on earth, I'm still a wanderer,
I have a tiny room of my own deep in my heart,
a room like an abyss where tears go in and light emerges.
My beginning, my conclusion is 'the room of my heart.'

Even if I was given everything in the world,
if there was no light in my heart's room,
and there was no true me there,
with what would I meet you and with what power would I set out?

Tonight, the room of my heart grows bright with a fire of love.

Cappadocia, Turkey, 2005.

내 마음의 방

지상에 집 한 채 갖지 못한 나는
아직도 유랑자로 떠다니는 나는
내 마음 깊은 곳에 나만의 작은 방이 하나 있어
눈물로 들어가 빛으로 나오는 심연의 방이 있어
나의 시작 나의 귀결은 '내 마음의 방'이니.

나에게 세상의 모든 것이 다 주어져도
내 마음의 방에 빛이 없고
거기 진정한 내가 없다면
나는 무엇으로 너를 만나고
무슨 힘으로 나아가겠는가.

이 밤, 사랑의 불로 내 마음의 방을 밝히네.

전쟁의 레바논에서, 박노해. Park Nohae in the battlefield of Lebanon, 2007.

박노해

1957 전라남도에서 태어났다. 16세에 상경해 낮에는 노동자로 일하고 밤에는 선린상고(야간)를 다녔다. **1984** 27살에 첫 시집 『노동의 새벽』을 출간했다. 이 시집은 독재 정권의 금서 조치에도 100만 부 가까이 발간되며 한국 사회와 문단을 충격으로 뒤흔들었다. 감시를 피해 사용한 박노해라는 필명은 '박해받는 노동자 해방'이라는 뜻으로, 이때부터 '얼굴 없는 시인'으로 알려졌다. **1989** 〈남한사회주의노동자동맹〉(사노맹)을 결성했다. **1991** 7년여의 수배 끝에 안기부에 체포, 24일간의 고문 후 '반국가단체 수괴' 죄목으로 사형이 구형되고 무기징역에 처해졌다. **1993** 감옥 독방에서 두 번째 시집 『참된 시작』을 출간했다. **1997** 옥중에세이 『사람만이 희망이다』를 출간했다. **1998** 7년 6개월 만에 석방되었다. 이후 민주화운동 유공자로 복권됐으나 국가보상금을 거부했다. **2000** "과거를 팔아 오늘을 살지 않겠다"며 권력의 길을 뒤로 하고 비영리단체 〈나눔문화〉(www.nanum.com)를 설립했다. **2003** 이라크 전쟁터에 뛰어들면서, 전 세계 가난과 분쟁 현장에서 평화활동을 이어왔다. **2010** 낡은 흑백 필름 카메라로 기록해온 사진을 모아 첫 사진전 「라 광야」展과 「나 거기에 그들처럼」展(세종문화회관)을 열었다. 12년 만의 시집 『그러니 그대 사라지지 말아라』를 출간했다. **2012** 나눔문화가 운영하는 〈라 카페 갤러리〉에서 상설 사진전을 개최하고 있다. 현재 20번째 전시를 이어가고 있으며, 총 33만 명의 관람객이 다녀갔다. **2014** 아시아 사진전 「다른 길」展(세종문화회관) 개최와 함께 『다른 길』을 출간했다. **2019** 박노해 사진에세이 시리즈 『하루』, 『단순하게 단단하게 단아하게』, 『길』을 출간했다. **2020** 첫 번째 시 그림책 『푸른 빛의 소녀가』를 출간했다. **2021** 『걷는 독서』를 출간했다. 감옥에서부터 30년간 써온 한 권의 책, '우주에서의 인간의 길'을 담은 사상서를 집필 중이다. '적은 소유로 기품 있게' 살아가는 〈참사람의 숲〉을 꿈꾸며, 오늘도 시인의 작은 정원에서 꽃과 나무를 심고 기르며 새로운 혁명의 길로 나아가고 있다.

매일, 사진과 글로 시작하는 하루 〈박노해의 걷는 독서〉 📷 park_nohae 🅕 parknohae

Park Nohae

Park Nohae is a legendary poet, photographer and revolutionary. He was born in 1957. While working as a laborer in his 20s, he began to reflect and write poems on the sufferings of the laboring class. He then took the pseudonym Park Nohae ("No" means "laborers," "Hae" means "liberation"). At the age of twenty-seven, Park published his first collection of poems, titled *The Dawn of Labor*, in 1984. Despite official bans, this collection sold nearly a million copies, and it shook Korean society with its shocking emotional power. Since then, he became an intensely symbolic figure of resistance, often called the "Faceless Poet." For several years the government authorities tried to arrest him in vain. He was finally arrested in 1991. After twenty-four days of investigation, with illegal torture, the death penalty was demanded for his radical ideology. He was finally sentenced to life imprisonment. After seven and a half years in prison, he was pardoned in 1998. Thereafter, he was reinstated as a contributor to the democratization movement, but he refused any state compensation. Park decided to leave the way for power, saying, "I will not live today by selling the past," and he established a nonprofit social movement organization "Nanum Munhwa," meaning "Culture of Sharing," (www.nanum.com) faced with the great challenges confronting global humanity. In 2003, right after the United States' invasion of Iraq, he flew to the field of war. Since then, he often visits countries that are suffering from war and poverty, such as Iraq, Palestine, Pakistan, Sudan, Tibet and Banda Aceh, in order to raise awareness about the situation through his photos and writings. He continues to hold photo exhibitions, and a total of 330,000 visitors have so far visited his exhibitions. He is writing a book of reflexions, the only such book he has written during the thirty years since prison, "The Human Path in Space." Dreaming of the Forest of True People, a life-community living "a graceful life with few possessions," the poet is still planting and growing flowers and trees in his small garden, advancing along the path toward a new revolution.

⟨Park Nohae's Reading while Walking Along⟩ ⓞ park_nohae ⨎ parknohae

저서

Books

박노해 사진에세이 시리즈

01 하루
02 단순하게 단단하게 단아하게
03 길

박노해 시인이 20여 년 동안 지상의 멀고 높은 길을 걸으며 기록해온 '유랑노트'이자 길 찾는 이에게 띄우는 두꺼운 편지. 각 권마다 37점의 흑백 사진과 캡션이 담겼다. 인생이란 한 편의 이야기이며 '에세이'란 그 이야기를 남겨놓는 것이니. 삶의 화두와도 같은 주제로 해마다 새 시리즈가 출간된다.

136p | 20,000KRW | 2019-2020

Park Nohae Photo Essay

01 One Day
02 Simply, Firmly, Gracefully
03 The Path

These are 'wandering notes' that the poet Park Nohae has recorded while walking along the Earth's long, high roads for over twenty years, a thick letter to those who seek for a path. Each volume contains 37 black-and-white photos and captions. Life is a story, and each of these 'essays' is designed to leave that story behind. A new volume is published every year like a topic of life.

걷는 독서

단 한 줄로도 충분하다! 한 권의 책이 응축된 듯한 423편의 문장들. 박노해 시인이 감옥 독방에 갇혀서도, 국경 너머 분쟁 현장에서도 멈추지 않은 일생의 의례이자 창조의 원천인 '걷는 독서'. 온몸으로 살고 사랑하고 저항해온 삶의 정수가 담긴 문장과 세계의 숨은 빛을 담은 컬러사진이 어우러져 언제 어디를 펼쳐봐도 지혜와 영감이 깃든다.

880p | 23,000KRW | 2021

Reading While Walking Along

One line is enough! 423 sentences, one whole book condensed into each sentence. 'Reading While Walking Along' is a lifelong ritual and source of creation by Park Nohae who never stopped, even after being confined in a prison cell or at the scene of conflicts beyond the border. The aphorisms that contain the essence of his life, in which he has lived, loved and resisted with his whole body, are harmonized with color photos that contain the hidden light of the world, delivering wisdom and inspiration wherever we open them.

푸른 빛의 소녀가

박노해 시인의 첫 번째 시 그림책. 저 먼 행성에서 찾아온 푸른 빛의 소녀와 지구별 시인의 가슴 시린 이야기. "지구에서 좋은 게 뭐죠?" 우주적 시야로 바라본 삶의 근본 물음과 아이들의 가슴에 푸른 빛의 상상력을 불어넣는 신비로운 여정이 펼쳐진다. "우리 모두는 별에서 온 아이들. 네 안에는 별이 빛나고 있어."(박노해)

72p | 19,500KRW | 2020

The Blue Light Girl

Poet Park Nohae's first Poetry Picture Book. The poignant tale of the Blue Light Girl visiting from a distant planet and a poet of Planet Earth. "What is good on Earth?" The fundamental question of life seen from a cosmic perspective. A mysterious journey inspiring an imagination of blue light in the heart of the children. "We are all children from the stars. Stars are shining in you."(Park Nohae)

그러니 그대 사라지지 말아라

영혼을 뒤흔드는 시의 정수. 저항과 영성, 교육과 살림, 아름다움과 혁명 그리고 사랑까지 붉디 붉은 304편의 시가 담겼다. 인생의 갈림길에서 길을 잃고 헤매는 순간마다 어디를 펼쳐 읽어도 좋을 책. 입소문만으로 이 시집을 구입한 6만 명의 독자가 증명하는 감동. "그러니 그대 사라지지 말아라" 그 한 마디가 나를 다시 살게 한다.

560p | 18,000KRW | 2010

So You Must Not Disappear

The essence of soul-shaking poetry! This anthology of 304 poems as red as its book cover, narrating resistance, spirituality, education, living, the beautiful, revolution and love. Whenever you're lost at a crossroads of your life, it will guide you with any page of it moving you. The intensity of moving is evidenced by the 60,000 readers who have bought this book only through word-of-mouth. "So you must not disappear". This one phrase makes me live again.

다른 길

"우리 인생에는 각자가 진짜로 원하는 무언가가 있다. 분명, 나만의 다른 길이 있다." 인디아에서 파키스탄, 라오스, 버마, 인도네시아, 티베트까지 지도에도 없는 마을로 떠나는 여행. 그리고 그 길의 끝에서 진정한 나를 만나는 새로운 여행에세이. '이야기가 있는 사진'이 한 걸음 다른 길로 우리를 안내한다.

352p | 19,500KRW | 2014

Another Way

"In our lives, there is something which each of us really wants. For me, certainly, I have my own way, different from others"(Park Nohae). From India, Pakistan, Laos, Burma, Indonesia to Tibet, a journey to villages nowhere to be seen on the map. And a new essay of meeting true self at the end of the road. 'Image with a story' guide us to another way.

노동의 새벽

1984년, 27살의 '얼굴 없는 시인'이 쓴 시집 한 권이 세상을 뒤흔들었다. 독재 정부의 금서 조치에도 100만 부 이상 발간되며 화인처럼 새겨진 불멸의 고전. 억압받는 천만 노동자의 영혼의 북소리로 울려퍼진 노래. "박노해는 역사이고 상징이며 신화다. 문학사적으로나 사회사적으로 우리는 그런 존재를 다시 만날 수 없을지 모른다."(문학평론가 도정일)

172p | 12,000KRW | 2014
30th Anniversary Edition

The Dawn of Labor

In 1984, an anthology of poems written by 27 years old 'faceless poet' shook Korean society. Recorded as a million seller despite the publication ban under military dictatorship, it became an immortal classic ingrained like a marking iron. It was a song echoing down with the throbbing pulses of ten million workers' souls. "Park Nohae is a history, a symbol, and a myth. All the way through the history of literature and society alike, we may never meet such a being again."(Doh Jeong-il, literary critic)

사람만이 희망이다

34살의 나이에 '불온한 혁명가'로 무기징역을 선고받은 박노해. 그가 1평 남짓한 독방에 갇혀 7년 동안 써내려간 옥중에세이. "90년대 최고의 정신적 각성"으로 기록되는 이 책은, 희망이 보이지 않는 오늘날 더 큰 울림으로 되살아난다. 살아있는 한 희망은 끝나지 않았다고. 다시, 사람만이 희망이라고.

320p | 15,000KRW | 2015

Only a Person is Hope

Park Nohae was sentenced to life imprisonment as a "rebellious revolutionary" when he was 34 years old. This essay written in solitary confinement measuring about three sq. m. for seven years. This book is recorded as the "best spiritual awakening in the 90s", is born again with the bigger impression today when there seems to be no hope at all. As long as you live, hope never ends. Again, only a person is hope.

내 작은 방

박노해 사진에세이 04

초판 2쇄 발행 2022년 1월 5일
초판 1쇄 발행 2022년 1월 4일

사진·글 박노해
번역 안선재
편집 김예슬, 윤지영
표지 디자인 홍동원
자문 이기명 아날로그 인화 유철수
제작 윤지혜 홍보 마케팅 이상훈
인쇄 자문 유화컴퍼니 인쇄 세현인쇄
제본 광성문화사 후가공 신화사금박

발행인 임소희
발행처 느린걸음
출판등록 2002년 3월 15일 제300-2009-109호
주소 서울시 종로구 사직로8길 34, 330호
전화 02-733-3773
팩스 02-734-1976
이메일 slow-walk@slow-walk.com
홈페이지 www.slow-walk.com
instagram.com/slow_walk_book

ⓒ 박노해 2022
ISBN 978-89-91418-32-5 04810
ISBN 978-89-91418-25-7 04810(세트)

번역자 안선재(안토니 수사)는 서강대학교 명예교수로
40권 이상의 한국 시와 소설의 영문 번역서를 펴냈다.

My Dear Little Room

Park Nohae Photo Essay 04

First edition, second publishing, Jan. 5, 2022
First edition, first publishing, Jan. 4, 2022

Photographed and Written by Park Nohae
Translated by Brother Anthony of Taizé
Edited by Kim Yeseul, Yun Jiyoung
Cover Designed by Hong Dongwon
Consulted by Lee Ki-Myoung
Photographic Analogue Prints by Yu Chulsu
Print Making by Yun Jihye
Marketing by Lee Sanghoon
Print Consulted by UHWACOMPANY

Publisher Im Sohee
Publishing Company Slow Walking
Address Rm330, 34, Sajik-ro 8-gil, Jongno-gu,
Seoul, Republic of Korea
Tel 82-2-7333773 Fax 82-2-7341976
E-mail slow-walk@slow-walk.com
Website www.slow-walk.com
instagram.com/slow_walk_book

ⓒ Park Nohae 2022
ISBN 978-89-91418-32-5 04810
ISBN 978-89-91418-25-7 04810(SET)

Translator An Sonjae(Brother Anthony of Taizé)
is professor emeritus at Sogang University.
He has published over forty volumes of
translations of Korean poetry and fiction.